SKYDIVING
... to the Extreme:

'Chute Roll

SHORT cuts
SERIES™

SKYDIVING
... to the Extreme:

'Chute Roll

Sigmund Brouwer

WORD Kids!®

WORD PUBLISHING
Dallas·London·Vancouver·Melbourne

Skydiving . . . to the Extreme: 'Chute Roll

Copyright © 1996 by Sigmund Brouwer.

Managing Editor: Laura Minchew
Project Editor: Beverly Phillips

Library of Congress Cataloging-in-Publication Data

Brouwer, Sigmund, 1959–
   Skydiving—to the extreme—'chute roll /
   Sigmund Brouwer.
      p. cm. — (Short cuts ; 3)
   "Word kids!"
   Summary: After saving the daughter of a wealthy
casino owner from being killed while skydiving,
sixteen-year-old Jeff Nichols is determined to find out
who wants her dead and why.
   ISBN 0-8499-3953-4 (trade paper)
   [1. Skydiving—Fiction. 2. Organized crime—
Fiction. 3. Christian life—Fiction. 4. Mystery and
detective stories.] I. Title. II. Series: Brouwer, Sigmund,
1959–   Short cuts ; 3.
PZ7.B79984Sk 1997
[Fic]—dc20

                                                96-38593
                                                    CIP
                                                     AC

Printed in the United States of America

97 98 99 00 OPM 9 8 7 6 5 4 3 2 1

To
Beverly Phillips—
Thanks for your help with all these books.
You've been cheerful and relentless!

Chapter One

I stood at the open door at the back of the airplane. I held on to the side of the doorway. I stared down at the desert. To the south, I could see Las Vegas. The buildings looked like little Lego blocks. I was 8,000 feet above the ground. That's nearly a mile and a half straight down. It's a long way to fall. Soon I would throw myself from the airplane into that mile and a half of empty space.

But not yet. I wasn't quite ready. There was one last thing to do. I needed to pray.

Some guys carry a lucky rabbit's foot.

Others knock on wood. Just about every-body has some way to deal with fear.

It is a simple fear. It is a fear that the para-chute won't open. And that the backup parachute won't open. If they both fail, you fall about the same speed as a piano . . . until spat—you're a blob of jam.

I closed my eyes to pray. I pray before every jump. I mean, I think it's better to believe in God than in a rabbit's foot. If I die, I'd rather meet Him than the ghost of a rabbit with no feet. Besides, how lucky could the rabbit be if someone had killed it and chopped its feet off?

"Dear God," I prayed, "thank you for let-ting this fear remind me that my life is always in your hands. Please keep me safe. Amen."

I opened my eyes again. The roar of the engines changed as the pilot turned to take the airplane over the target far below. The wind noise rushed through my helmet. I shook from the force of the air that pushed over the airplane wings and into the door-way.

"Hey, Jeff!"

The shout came from a girl standing right

behind me in the airplane. Sabella Scanelli. She's one of the best. My main competition. She and I were the only ones going up for this jump.

I turned my head slightly. There wasn't much time before I needed to jump.

"Yeah?" I shouted back.

"Betcha a hundred dollars I land closer!"

She meant closer to the target on the ground. We were both training for the biggest parachute event of the year.

Instead of answering with another shout, I shook my head no.

"Chicken?" There was a big grin across her suntanned face.

She knew I wasn't chicken. I just didn't have her kind of money. Her father owned a casino in Las Vegas. A long, shiny black car brought her to the airport to jump. It took her away again as soon as she was finished. Me? I wasn't rich. I had to work at the flight school to pay for my jumps.

"Chickens don't fly!" I shouted above the wind. "But I do!"

I pushed myself into all that empty air.

Chapter Two

I love the feeling of letting the wind sweep me into a free fall. It is as close to flying as a person can get.

Face down, I spread my legs and arms. Although I was falling at more than 100 miles an hour, I was still so high that the ground didn't seem to get any closer. At least not yet. But if my parachute didn't open . . .

Far below me I saw the brown of the desert. The airport runway was a dark slash of pavement across it. Farther away a large circle of red and white marked the target.

Soon enough, I would have to concentrate on getting my angle right.

For now, though, I was having fun. I leaned one way. Then the other. I moved my arms and swooped like a hawk. In free fall, without an open parachute, you can twist and turn in the wind.

Finally, I pulled on my rip cord.

I held my breath.

Although I have jumped more than 200 times, pulling the rip cord is the one thing that makes me nervous. For a few seconds, I always wonder if my 'chute will open. In my nightmares, I'm falling toward the ground. In my nightmares, I have two or three minutes to watch it rush toward me. In my nightmares, I have all that time to wonder what it will feel like to smash into the ground.

I held my breath and counted the seconds. One, two, three . . .

Bang!

My shoulder straps jerked me as the 'chute opened wide. It slowed my fall from a 120 miles per hour to 10 miles per hour. It slowed me so quickly that it seemed to yank me upward, like a giant hand pulling me from above.

I started to breathe again. Now all I had to do was guide myself toward the target as I floated downward.

I looked over my shoulder to see where Sabella was. I spotted her about a minute behind me. She was a dark shape against the pale blue sky.

I checked the ground.

I checked Sabella.

I checked the ground again.

I checked Sabella. And nearly screamed.

Her 'chute had tangled!

The strings of the parachute were all wound together, and it could not fill with air.

She tumbled toward me. Because I was floating and she was in free fall, she gained on me like a rock.

I saw her pull the breakaway cord and release her main 'chute. She yanked at her second rip cord to open her reserve parachute.

Nothing happened. No 'chute opened behind her.

I couldn't hear her scream, but her mouth was wide open in terror.

A second later, she flashed past me on her way toward death.

There was only one thing to do. I had to cut myself loose from my parachute.

Chapter Three

I arched my back. If you don't do a breakaway right, you get thrown into a spin. Once I was level, I pulled on the breakaway handle.

It took less than a second to lose my main 'chute.

I fell toward the ground. I dropped my head and pointed my arms straight down into a dive position.

Sabella was falling belly first. She had her arms and legs wide to slow herself as much as possible. You've got a one in a million chance to survive a free fall, but she was trying.

In my dive, I started to gain on her. By cutting through the air in a dive, you can go from 120 miles per hour up to 200 miles per hour.

She was a little ahead and to the left. I kicked a leg out to change my direction. I aimed straight at her.

The wind screamed against my face and goggles.

Twenty seconds later, I had cut the distance in half. Ten seconds later, I had cut it in half again.

But the ground was getting closer and closer. I could see the cross-like shadows of cactus trees. If I didn't reach Sabella soon . . .

Five, four, three, two . . .

Her dark hair was flapping from beneath her helmet like a blanket. It almost whipped in my face as I reached her. I had to time it just right. I flung out my hand and grabbed her ankle.

She screamed.

"Don't panic," I shouted.

With both hands, I pulled myself up her body. The rushing wind tried to tear us apart. But I held on.

The ground was closer and closer still.

Finally, I yanked the second rip cord on my parachute. It was for my backup 'chute. I prayed it would open. . . .

As I waited those awful few seconds, I wrapped my arms around Sabella. I hugged her tight against my chest. I needed to be holding her with all my strength.

My 'chute flopped open and yanked at us.

I held tight. We were maybe a thousand feet off the ground and still traveling fast. Would there be enough time for the single parachute to slow down the weight of two people?

Chapter Four

Roll left when we hit!" I shouted into Sabella's helmet. "Hear me? Roll left!"

She nodded.

I would roll to the right. The last thing we needed to do was crash into each other on the ground. That could break ribs or arms or legs.

We both straightened, pointing our feet toward the ground.

I could see the shadows of rocks. I also saw something else, and I didn't like it.

Cactuses. Big cactuses. In a big patch. Right below us.

If it were just me, I'd be able to steer by pulling on the parachute cords. But with Sabella in my arms, we had no choice but to drift where the 'chute took us.

We fell into the cactus patch.

Cactus needles tore at my face and hands as I rolled. I stood and looked behind me. My 'chute was shredded.

Sabella was just getting to her feet.

"You all right?" I asked.

"Except for all the cactus needles in my . . ." She pointed at her backside. "I won't be able to sit for a week."

Now that it was all over, I began to feel the cactus needles in my own body.

"Me neither," I said.

"It could be worse," she said. She took off her helmet and shook her hair loose around her face. "I could be a blob of jelly somewhere on the desert floor."

She took a step toward me. "You saved my life."

"It's not a big deal," I said. It wasn't. If I hadn't been able to reach her in time, I could still have saved myself with my backup 'chute.

"I'd hug you," she said, "but with all these needles, it would hurt both of us."

"That's all right," I said. I pointed behind her at a trail of rising dust. "Besides, it looks like we have company."

She frowned at the sight of a big black car driving toward us at a high speed.

"Your dad?" I asked. Sabella never hung around the flight school. The black car was the one I'd seen picking her up and dropping her off.

"No," she said. Her frown stayed in place. "My bodyguards."

Bodyguards?

The car reached us. It skidded sideways as it stopped. Dust choked us.

The car had smoked-glass windows. I couldn't see inside.

Two guys jumped out, one from each side. Both were big. Both wore dark blue suits.

"Miss Sabella, you hurt?" the driver asked. He had a pair of binoculars hanging from his neck. "We saw what happened."

"I'm standing, aren't I?" she said. "Thanks to Jeff."

The driver turned his face toward me. It was not a pretty face. His nose was crooked. He had a scar across his chin.

"What's your name?"

"Jeff Nichols," I said.

"You done good," he told me. "Mr. Scanelli will be pleased."

The other guy was just as ugly. He had a cell phone pressed to his head. He walked over to the first guy and gave him the phone.

"I've told the boss what happened. He wants to talk to you."

The driver took the phone.

"Yes, Mr. Scanelli," he said into the phone. He walked away from us to talk. I couldn't hear the rest of what he said. I didn't want to. All of this was weird.

The second guy spoke to Sabella. "Would you get into the car now, Miss Scanelli?"

"If I don't?"

"You know your father has told you to listen to us," the bodyguard said.

"Well, you weren't much good to me in the sky."

"Miss Scanelli, if you don't get inside, I'll have to carry you inside. Would you like that?"

Sabella did not say anything. She marched to the car. I heard her say ouch as she sat down. Cactus needles.

She slammed the door behind her.

The bodyguard watched me.

It was hot. My body hurt in a hundred places from cactus needles. It was about a mile back to the airport. I wanted to get back soon.

"Any chance I can catch a ride with you guys?" I asked.

The ugly bodyguard didn't answer.

Fine, I told myself. I had two legs. I didn't like the looks of these guys anyway. Besides, I had to get back to the flight school to write an accident report. It's not good when parachutes don't open.

I started to walk.

"Stay," the guy said.

Stay? Was I some sort of dog?

That made me mad. I kept walking.

I never knew a guy so big could move so fast. Especially in a suit.

I heard the crunch of his shoes on the rocks and sand of the desert. Before I could turn to look, he was in front of me. He grabbed my flight jacket and lifted me off the ground.

Chapter Five

Stay," he said again.

I'm not small. Up close, though, this guy made me feel like a six-year-old kid.

"Okay," I said. "I'll stay."

He set me down. He stared at me. Small beads of sweat popped out on the skin of his face.

He didn't smile. I decided I should just keep my mouth shut and wait.

Finally, the driver came over. He snapped the cell phone shut and handed it to the second guy.

The driver looked at me. "Mr. Scanelli is

very pleased that you saved his daughter's life. He wishes to reward you."

"It's all right," I said. "I don't need a reward."

"Don't say no to Mr. Scanelli. It's not a good idea."

The driver reached inside his suit jacket. He pulled out a long, flat wallet. He opened the wallet and took out some bills.

"Take this," he said, handing me the money.

"I told you already. I don't need a reward."

The second guy grabbed my wrist and raised my arm toward the money. He squeezed hard. It hurt. I got the hint. I took the money.

"Count it," the driver said.

They were hundred dollar bills. I counted twenty of them. That was two thousand dollars.

"Mr. Scanelli also wants you to do something else for him."

"What is it?" I asked.

"He wants you to keep this to yourself."

"I can't," I said. "I have to file a report. I work at the flight school. They have to know about the accident. They have to look into it and see what went wrong."

The driver stepped right up to me. He looked down his crooked nose at me.

"Don't you hear good?" he asked. His breath smelled like garlic.

"Yes," I said. "But—"

"Mr. Scanelli always gets what he wants," the driver said. "Let me put it this way. If you file a report, I will break both your knees."

The big, ugly man patted my face. "Not only that, kid. If you even tell a single person about this, I will break both your knees."

He grabbed my chin and forced me to look straight into his flat, black eyes.

"Look at me, kid. See how serious I am? Do you think I'm joking?"

"Um, no."

"Say it again, kid. Tell me you know I'll break your legs if anyone hears about what happened up there."

I believed him. Looking into his face, I believed he was the kind of guy who would break a person's legs. Or do worse stuff. I told him I believed him.

"Good," he said. He let go of me.

The two of them walked back to the car. They drove away.

I stood there with two thousand dollars in my hand. And with legs so weak from fear I could hardly stand.

If this was what happened when Mr. Scanelli was pleased, I didn't want to find out what would happen if he was mad.

Chapter Six

I was dreaming about a woodpecker. It was sitting on my head and trying to dig into my brain. When I woke up, I realized the knock-knock sound was not a woodpecker. The knock-knock came from the front door.

I looked at my alarm clock. It was seven thirty.

Knock. Knock. Knock.

Who would be knocking at the door this early? Even though my folks had already left for work, the sun was barely up.

I put on a robe and stumbled to the door.

I looked through the peephole of the front door.

Sabella Scanelli!

I opened the door. She stepped inside before I could ask her to come in. She shut the door behind her.

"Jeff," she said. Her long dark hair was tied back. She wore jeans and a leather jacket over a T-shirt. Her face was beautiful.

"Uh-huh," I said without opening my mouth. I hadn't even brushed my teeth. I didn't want to blast her with morning breath.

"Sit down," I said, covering my mouth. I pointed at an armchair.

I slipped into my room to put on blue jeans and a clean T-shirt. I went to the bathroom and brushed my teeth and splashed water on my hair. As I combed my hair back, I stared at the mirror to see myself as Sabella would see me.

My blue eyes looked back at me. They were in a face still puffy from sleep. I decided there wasn't much to be impressed with. I am not ugly, but on the other hand, movie people will never chase me down to make me a star.

When my ordinary hair was combed

neatly above my ordinary face, I went back out to my visitor.

"Good morning," I said.

"I'm sorry it's so early," she answered.

"That's okay. My parents are up and out already."

"How old are you?" she asked.

"Sixteen."

"It seems like you have a lot of freedom."

"My parents trust me," I said. "We talk a lot about the future, when I'll have a place of my own. They want me to be ready to make it on my own."

"You're lucky," she said. "I wish I could look forward to something like that."

"Who's stopping you?"

She laughed. It was a sad laugh. "Think of a bird in a cage made of gold. That's me."

"I don't get it," I said.

She stared at me for a few minutes as if she were deciding something. "You don't want to know," she finally said. "Trust me."

She stood. "Anyway, last night I called the flight school for your schedule. You work early today."

"Yes," I said.

"So I'm here hoping I can get a ride with

you," she said. "It took me nearly two hours to walk here. But the airport is so far out of town it would take most of the rest of the day to get there."

"But what about—"

"My bodyguards and the big black car?" she asked.

I nodded.

"That's why I'm here," she said. "I ran away from them."

Chapter Seven

Fifteen minutes later, we were standing on the street in the bright Las Vegas sunshine. There were several cars parked there. None of them were mine.

"All I have is a motorcycle," I told Sabella. "Is that okay?"

"As long as it gets us there. I want to jump today."

I unlocked my helmet from the motorbike. I had a spare helmet for her.

We got on the motorbike. It's not too big—500 cc—and it uses a lot less gas than a car. I try to save all my money for skydiving.

I had already put the two thousand dollars in my savings account.

Sabella held on as I pulled out of the parking lot. I liked that. It seemed like she wanted to be my friend. Which was fine with me.

My home is on the outskirts of town. It takes a bunch of winding streets to get to the main road. I noticed a square brown car in my side mirrors. At first, it didn't bother me.

A few minutes later, it did. Just because it was still following us. There wasn't much traffic. It looked like the driver was doing his best to keep one or two cars between us.

We reached the main road.

I gunned the motorbike. The brown car sped up and stayed with us.

I slowed down.

It slowed down.

"Sabella," I shouted above the wind noise.

She leaned forward to hear better.

"There are two guys following us in a brown car. Do you know them?"

"No," she said.

"Do you want them to know where we're going?"

"No," she said.

"Me neither."

"Hang on tight," I said. "Lean with me into the turn!"

She wrapped her arms around my waist.

I spun a U-turn and drove straight back the way we'd come.

As we passed them going the opposite direction, I got a better look at their faces. They wore brown suits. They had crew cuts. Dark sunglasses hid their eyes.

Both of them snapped their heads to look at us.

I laughed.

"We're on our own," I told Sabella. "No worries now!"

Which, as I found out later, was one of the dumbest things I could have said.

Chapter Eight

The flight school is a big old building just off one of the airport runways. It's not much of a building. Just a wide-open warehouse with room to park some planes. It also has some rooms and offices at the front. Of course, it's not much of an airport either. The big airport in Las Vegas is where all the jets come in. This airport is way out in the desert. It has a couple of small runways for small propeller airplanes.

I punched the time clock to start work.

Sabella went to the pop machine and got us some colas.

She found me at one of the tables, packing parachutes.

"Here," she said, handing me a cola, "thanks for the lift."

"No problem," I said. "Are you heading up soon?"

"Yeah," she said. "Spike is going to make the runs for me."

Spike is somewhere between forty years old and sixty years old. It's hard to tell exactly. He usually has so much engine grease on his face that the wrinkles are filled in. Spike has been a pilot forever. He wears old coveralls that are dirtier than his face and hands. When he's not flying, he sits in the coffee room and chews tobacco. He spits the juice into a pop can. He's the first one here every day and the last one to leave. Everyone calls him Spike because he is bald. Except for the one short black hair that sticks up from the middle of his head.

"Take this for your first jump," I said, handing her a parachute. "I packed it myself."

"Thank you."

I pointed at a mess of rolled-up parachute in the corner. "That's yours from yesterday.

I'm going to see if I can figure out what happened."

She shuddered. "I'm trying not to think about yesterday."

"Are you scared?" I asked.

"I've never been more scared," she said. "That's why I snuck out of the house this morning. I have to prove to myself I can still do it."

Her eyes were wide as she spoke. "You see, my father told me I could never jump again. He's too afraid it might happen again."

"I can understand how he feels. People who don't jump do get nervous thinking about what we do."

"No!"

She surprised me with her sudden anger.

"No," she said again. Softer. "Jeff, my father has controlled everything I do since I was very little. Skydiving is my way of breaking away. I fought and fought just to get the chance to do it. If I quit now, it's like letting him run my life forever."

"From my experience," I said, "parents usually know what they're doing."

"I'm not going to explain my home life to you," she said. Her mouth was tight with anger. "I spend enough time in that gold cage."

"But—"

"But nothing. I've probably already said too much. If I tell you anything else, you might get hurt. Bad. So no more questions, okay? Leave me alone."

I snapped my mouth shut.

Spike stuck his dirty face through the doorway. "Plane's ready," he said.

Sabella marched away from me for her first jump of the day.

I went back to work. I tried to make sense of what she had said, but I couldn't figure out a thing. A half hour later, when I got around to looking at her parachute, I did figure out one thing.

And it made me very afraid.

Chapter Nine

I was waiting for her as she drifted down. She and I both competed in the accuracy event. The target is set on the ground near the runway, so you don't have far to walk after you land.

Think of trying to drop marbles into a tin can. From the top of a twenty-story building. That's what it's like for us. In the middle of the target is a small plastic disc. It's only four inches wide. Hardly bigger than your hand. You are supposed to land right on top of it with one foot.

That's the hard part.

It helps that parachutes have steering cables. You can turn with them. You can slow down with them. Or, by loosening them, you can speed up. So, even with a wind, you have a good chance of hitting the target.

One guy did it 105 times in a row to win a world championship. I'm good. Sabella's good. But we're not that good. That's one of the reasons we practice.

As I watched her come down, I admired her great form. Her eyes were on nothing but the target. Her hands adjusted the steering cable. The nylon 'chute above her worked like the wings of a slow airplane.

Just above the ground, she reached with her right foot. It landed square on the target, and she touched the earth like a feather. Not bad for someone who had aimed for the target from more than a mile away.

Sabella rolled forward and got to her feet. She unsnapped herself from her shoulder straps and stepped away from her parachute.

She grinned. "Checking out the person who's going to take first place?"

I grinned back. "I'd need a mirror for that."

"Very funny," she said.

I could tell she was in a better mood. "Not afraid of jumping?"

"Not afraid," she said. "It was great."

"Good." I looked at my feet. I didn't know how to tell her what I needed to tell her.

"Jeff," she said, "I'm sorry for snapping at you this morning. What's happening to me is not your fault. I shouldn't take it out on you."

"That's why I'm here," I said. "I'm wondering what's happening."

She frowned. "Really, it would be better for you if you didn't know."

"Thanks," I said. "But maybe I already know more than I should."

"What do you mean?"

"Your parachute," I said. "The one that tangled on you yesterday. It wasn't an accident."

Her mouth opened and she tried to speak. But no words came.

"I know you've been talking about learning to pack your own 'chute," I said. "And I have a good reason you should start soon. The cords were tangled because someone packed it wrong. And your backup 'chute didn't open because the rip cord was cut."

I took a breath. "It's your own 'chute. Not a rental. Not one of the flight school's. Unless I'm wrong, someone tried to kill you yesterday."

Chapter Ten

I had a jump of my own later that morning. After talking to Sabella, I packed my own parachute carefully. Very carefully. For all I knew, someone wanted other people dead too.

It was strange enough that someone had tried to kill Sabella. It was stranger that she wouldn't talk to me about it. She wouldn't guess why someone might want her dead.

That left me guessing on my own.

I knew that Sabella never packed her own 'chute. Strangers weren't allowed to wander around inside. That meant someone at the flight school had done it.

There was a binder where people signed off whenever they packed a parachute. The binder showed me that Bill Blundel had packed her 'chute yesterday. But I didn't think he had wrecked it. First of all, he wasn't the type. Second, it would have been really stupid on his part. Why wreck someone's 'chute and then sign the binder so that everyone knew it was you?

No, I had to believe someone had taken her 'chute after Bill packed it. That still left me the two questions. Who? Why?

Until I knew, I couldn't trust anyone. After packing my parachute, I made sure I didn't leave it in a place where someone could do something to it. As it turned out, though, my parachute was the least of my problems on my jump.

Chapter Eleven

Just after noon, the two big guys came by in their long black car to get Sabella. She hadn't told them where to find her. They'd figured it out on their own. Not that she cared. From what Sabella had told me, she was just trying to prove that she had a right to make her own decisions.

After the car drove away in the shimmering desert heat, I had my chance to jump. Spike took me high, circled the valley, and flew away as soon as I jumped. I didn't even hear the buzzing of his airplane as my body screamed down through the air.

I dove and swooped like a bird. I spun circles. I did somersaults.

Finally, at 2,000 feet, I yanked on the rip cord to open my 'chute. As always, I held my breath and counted. One, two, three . . .

Bang!

The parachute jerked me as it caught air. I relaxed and let myself dangle for a few moments. I couldn't wait long, though. There was a wind pushing me crossways. I wasn't surprised. As the heat of the day builds, the air gets bumpy. Often it flows over the Spring Mountains to the west and right across the flat of the valley.

I began to steer the 'chute. But I didn't want to oversteer. It is easy to find ways to speed up toward the target as you land. It is almost impossible to drift back to it if you have gone too far.

At the same time, I allowed myself to enjoy the view. It is a great feeling to hang alone in the sky, miles above the ground. I'm always sad when I have to touch down to earth.

I looked to my left and saw Charleston Peak across the valley. I looked to my right and saw Lake Mead. It filled the valley of the Colorado River behind the Hoover Dam. I looked down and saw a ribbon of highway across the browns and reds of desert.

Closer and closer I drifted to the ground. When your parachute is open, there is no wind noise. You are moving with the wind. It was peaceful and beautiful.

Until I heard a zing. Then a loud echoing crack.

I didn't understand at first.

Another zing. Another loud echoing crack.

What was going on?

My 'chute seemed to spill some air. I had to steer to make up for it.

Zing. Crack.

It sounded . . . like . . . a . . . rifle. The zing was the bullet, outracing the sound of the crack of the rifle.

I looked up. There were three holes in my 'chute. Holes where the sky was bright against the silky red of the parachute fabric. The holes weren't big enough to wreck the parachute. But the holes were bad news.

Someone was shooting at me!

I looked down. I saw nobody.

Zing. Crack.

Somewhere in the desert bush there was a person hidden. A person with a rifle. A person aiming at me. A person who wanted to punch holes in my body with pieces of lead that moved faster than the speed of sound.

And all I could do was hang in the sky, a big, fat juicy target.

Chapter Twelve

I found out who the shooter was that night. I had landed without any holes in my body to leak blood into my jumpsuit. I had walked the short distance to the airport runway without any more shots taken at me. All that had been damaged was my parachute. Of course, my racing heart had put on a dozen miles of fear. But I'd lived to work the rest of the day.

I left the flight school on my motorbike at 6:30 and got home at 7:00. It was there that I found out who the shooter was.

As I locked my helmet to my motorbike, a

big man appeared and stood with his arms folded across his chest.

"Happy to be alive, kid?" he asked. He was ten years older than me. He was completely bald, as if he shaved his head. He had a goatee and a face like a bowling ball. He wore a dark suit.

I pretended I hadn't heard him. This dude was scary.

"I'm talking to you kid. Happy to be alive?"

There was no one else nearby to help me. I began to walk away. I was ready to run.

"I could have shot you dead, kid. Those holes in your parachute were just to get your attention."

I turned around.

He laughed. "Surprised I'm telling you? Not that it will do any good. You don't know who I am. And it's your word against mine. But trust me, I was the guy with the rifle."

"I've never seen you before. Why would you want to shoot me?"

"Shoot *at* you. Remember that. If I wanted to shoot you, you'd be dead."

"Why?" I asked. My mouth was as dry as desert sand. The day before, a big goon had promised he would break my legs. This goon had already shot at me. What was going on?

"It's a warning, kid. Keep out of it."

"It?"

"Don't play dumb. We know the Scanelli girl came to you for help this morning. You get one chance. This one. If you help her again, we'll leave you in the desert as food for buzzards."

"But—"

"But nothing. That stunt diving you did yesterday to grab her in the air. Don't do it again."

"Stunt diving? She was going to die!"

"Exactly. Her old man double-crossed us, and that's the price she's going to pay."

He smiled. A gold tooth flashed at me. "See, kid, it's like this. No matter how long it takes, no matter where she goes, we're going to get her."

"If it's her father that—"

"Her old man that did us wrong? The idiot. He's in the mob. He knows what happens to people who squeal to the feds. His trouble is that he thought he could outsmart us. That we wouldn't know who did the singing. What he doesn't know is that we have someone close to him."

Mob? Feds? Her father was a part of the Mafia? He was talking to the FBI? Telling them about other mob people?

"Mob," I said out loud. As if that would make this real.

"Now I see you're following me kid. He's already begun to sing his little song to the feds. But we're not going to let him get away with it. Since we can only kill him once, we want to hurt him through his daughter. If she goes, every day for the rest of his life he's gonna regret his mistake."

I was confused. Very confused. The big guy probably saw it on my face.

"What I'm telling you, kid, is simple. Sabella's going to die. You can't stop us. You have to decide whether you want to die too. Stay away, and you live. Make a move, and you can join her."

His smile got bigger. "Next time you go on a jump with her, you let her fall. Got that? If you get in our way again, we'll be dropping you from 10,000 feet. And I promise you won't have no fancy parachute on your back."

I couldn't answer. I could hardly believe this was happening. How can you answer when it doesn't seem real?

"Tomorrow," he said, "we're going to put her in a 'chute roll."

'Chute roll. It's a freak accident. Something that happens if an airplane passes too close by. The wake of the air flips you up and into your parachute. You roll. You die.

"Why am I telling you this?" he asked. "It's part of the price you pay for getting into business that don't belong to you. We'd kill you, too, but one accident is enough. Any more, and people might look into it too close."

He started to back away. His evil smile did not change. "So the price you pay, kid, is that you get to watch her die."

Chapter Thirteen

My parents had gone out to dinner and a movie. Which left me alone. Too alone. Inside I locked the doors and set chairs in front of them to stop a Mafia guy from crashing through. That's how scared I was.

I sat on the floor and thought about what I had just learned.

I wondered if I should go to the police. But would they believe me? And if they did, they'd protect Sabella. Then the mob people would know I had tried to help her. Then I would be dropped from an airplane without a parachute. And my nightmares about falling would come true.

I wondered if I should call the FBI. Except—even if I knew who to call—I'd have the same problems as calling the police.

No, I knew I had to speak to Sabella without the gold-toothed guy finding out. Then Sabella could protect herself. And I could stay out of it.

I walked into the kitchen and grabbed the phone book off the counter. The goon with the gold tooth was scary. But stupid. All I had to do was call Sabella. Who would ever know I had helped her?

After a few minutes, I realized maybe the gold-toothed guy wasn't so dumb. I couldn't find any Scanellis in the phone book. When I called information for the Scanelli number, the operator told me it was unlisted. When I thought about it, it made sense. If I were a Mafia guy, I wouldn't want many people to know how to get ahold of me.

There was one last thing I could try. I could sneak to her house and try to talk to her without being seen. Only problem was, I didn't know her address.

I called the flight school. No surprise,

Spike answered. It seemed like he lived there.

"Spike," I said, "can you go to the files and find an address for me?"

"What's it worth?" he asked over the telephone.

"Well . . ." His answer had surprised me.

"Ten bucks," he said.

"Ten bucks?"

"If you don't want to, don't worry about it. If you have time to waste, you can always come out here yourself."

"Ten bucks," I said. "Get me Sabella Scanelli's address. It should be on the forms she signed to skydive."

As I waited, I thought about Spike. Funny how little things say so much about a person.

Spike got back on the phone a few minutes later. "201 Palmetto Place."

"Thanks," I said.

"Forget the thanks. Give me the ten spot next time you see me. Or else."

I was tired of threats. I hung up on him.

Chapter Fourteen

I found Sabella Scanelli's home without any problem. My problem was the front gates. She lived in a mansion, set far back from the road.

I parked my motorcycle on the street.

My watch showed 8:00. It was dark. My shadow from the streetlights was long in front of me as I walked to the gates.

I stood, wondering what to do. I mean, you just don't knock on the gate and expect someone to answer the door.

"Who are you?" a voice asked. It sounded like someone was talking through a tin can.

I finally saw the speaker behind an overgrown bush. On the other side of the gate. Right beside it was a video camera.

"I'm a friend of Sabella Scanelli."

"What is your name?" the voice asked.

"Jeff Nichols."

"Is she expecting you?"

"No," I said. "Can you tell her it's important?"

No answer.

I stood there longer. Much longer. I hoped the person on the other end of the speaker had actually gone to look for Sabella. For all I knew, I could be standing here all night.

I looked around as I waited.

A driveway on the other side of the gate led up to the mansion. It was a three-story building with big windows.

The grounds of the mansion were bigger than a dozen football fields. There were palm trees all over. There were small ponds. There were statues lit by floodlights.

It looked like a nice place to live. But it wouldn't be worth it if you had to be part of the mob to live there. Or maybe to die there.

I heard footsteps.

Way ahead, a man was walking down the driveway toward me. In the dark, I couldn't see his face. All I could see was the outline of his body. It was a big body.

The footsteps grew louder as he got closer.

I felt chills. If Mr. Scanelli was part of the mob, there was a good chance this guy was too. I remembered the movies I had seen about gangsters. Would this guy pull out a machine gun and spray me with bullets?

Closer. Closer. His face was completely in shadow. He didn't say anything.

Finally, about ten feet away, he stepped into a pool of light from a lamp near the driveway.

I nearly fell backward in surprise.

It was the man with the gold tooth. The man who had told me he would kill me if I tried to help Sabella.

I remembered what he had said to me about Mr. Scanelli. *His trouble is that he thought he could outsmart us. That we wouldn't know who did the singing. What he doesn't know is that we have someone close to him.*

That someone close was this man with the gold tooth.

"Didn't listen, did you kid?" He pulled a

pistol from his jacket. "Listen now. If she doesn't die tomorrow, you die with her."

He pointed the gun at my head and pulled the trigger.

Click.

He lowered the gun and laughed at me. "Next time, expect a bullet."

He lifted the gun and pointed it at my head again. "You've got five seconds to run. Otherwise I pull the trigger again. And this time, it won't click dry."

I ran.

Chapter Fifteen

A block away from the Scanelli mansion, a pair of headlights turned on behind me. The lights were bright. They blinded me when they reflected in my motorcycle mirrors.

I gave the bike gas.

The headlights stayed with me.

I turned hard at the next corner.

The headlights stayed with me.

The streets were winding streets, up in the hills. I couldn't go too fast.

I also had no idea where I was going. All I wanted was to keep distance between me and the headlights.

I turned corner after corner, trying to lose the headlights. Nothing worked.

Three minutes later, I hit a dead end. I could see where the street ended a hundred yards ahead. I spun my bike around and faced the headlights.

For a moment, I stayed where I was. I gunned the motorcycle engine and got ready.

I knew what I had to do. I had to run at the car as fast as possible. I had to fake going one way, but take the other way. Once I was past the car, I could escape.

The car screeched to a stop about fifty yards away.

Both doors opened.

In the glare of the headlights, I saw very little. There was a man behind each door, facing me.

"Freeze!" a voice shouted. "FBI!"

Chapter Sixteen

The next morning, I got to the flight school early. I went into the office and checked to see when Sabella was scheduled to jump. She had booked a flight at 10:00 with Smitty.

Smitty was a good guy and a good pilot. He was in his thirties. He was tall and skinny and was always smiling.

I knew which plane Smitty would be taking. That helped. I had a lot to do to get ready.

A little under two hours later, when Sabella stepped into the back of the airplane, I was waiting for her.

"Jeff," she said. "What's this? I had this flight booked just for me."

Now, at least, I knew how her dad was able to afford her solo jumps. The rest of us always had to go up with other people.

"We need to talk," I told her. I strapped myself into the seat beside her.

Smitty, in the front, fired up the airplane engines.

"If you're here to talk, why are you in your jumpsuit?" she asked. "Why do you have your 'chute?"

"That's part of what we have to talk about."

Smitty had a headset on and was talking to the radar crew. He taxied the airplane onto the runway. Smitty couldn't hear us, so I raised my voice above the noise of the engines.

"Aren't you worried that someone might try to kill you again?" I asked.

"It's none of your business," she said. Her dark eyes became darker with anger.

"Yes, it is," I told her. "There's a guy who works for your dad. A guy with a gold tooth."

"How do you know?" She looked a little frightened.

"Last night he told me he would kill me. That's why this is my business."

She stared at me. The airplane began to pick up speed.

"I'm sorry," she said. I didn't really hear her, though. I was reading her lips because the airplane was loud and shaking.

I moved my head closer to her. Neither of us had our helmets on yet, so we were able to shout in each other's ears.

"I know your father is part of the mob," I told her. "The mob knows he's talked to the FBI. The mob wants to kill you for it."

I explained everything to her. The airplane reached 5,000 feet by the time I finished.

I was surprised she didn't look scared. I had just told her that she was going to be murdered. Today.

"Jeff," she said a few minutes later. "All of this is a risk my father and I discussed. He hates what he does. He wants out. He was getting ready for us to leave the country and live under different names. The only way the FBI would help was if he gave them some information first."

She shook her head sadly. "Ronnie? The guy with the gold tooth? He's been like part of the family for years. I would never have guessed that he would do this to us. What a pity."

We were now at 7,000 feet. The desert was open and wide below us.

I turned sideways in my seat and shook her shoulders. "Sabella. Hellooooo. What do you mean, a pity? They want to kill you. When you jump."

"Yeah," she said. "You already told me."

"And?"

"We're marked now. No one escapes once the mob puts the word out for a hit," she said. Sadness filled her face. "And we were only a week away from leaving the country."

"You're just giving up," I said.

She turned to face me. "You want to know why I jump? Freedom. I can't help what my father did with the mob. With all that money, we're both like birds in a cage. I can't leave him, though. He's my father. I love him. My mother's been dead a long time. He needs me. The sky is the only place I feel free."

"What does that have to do with giving up?" I asked.

"If I jump, I'm not giving up. If I have to die, I'm going to do it my way. Not running and hiding like some mouse in a dark room."

We talked some more. I suggested a partner jump.

"No, it's too risky," she said. But I was determined to help if I could.

"My mind's made up," I told her "I'm jumping."

Chapter Seventeen

My partner and I fell toward the ground. We were holding hands. In parachuting, there are other events besides target. During free fall, before their 'chutes open, divers hold hands and move around. Teams make different shapes in the air.

It didn't look that strange then, when I jumped with my partner. And I knew I'd have to worry about how we looked. Ronnie, the gold-toothed guy, had said the 'chute roll would happen today. That meant a pilot and an airplane would be diving out of the sky to roll Sabella. That also meant the pilot—whoever he was—would be watching closely.

As always, the ground hardly seemed to get closer. From 8,000 feet, the free-fall part seems much slower than it is.

My partner and I twisted and turned together. I made sure I held on tight to my partner's wrists.

I held off on pulling the rip cord. A 'chute roll could only happen if the parachute was open. The longer I waited, the better.

I felt the air push at the skin and flesh of my face. Sometimes, when I'm in a goofy mood, I let my lips flap in the wind. This, though, was not a time to be goofy.

Six thousand feet and still dropping like an anvil.

Then I saw the airplane. It was a speck, but growing larger.

I waited.

Five thousand feet.

The airplane headed straight for us.

I pushed away, yanking my partner's rip cord. The 'chute trailed out, then opened. I dropped away from my partner, still in free fall.

I kept looking up, getting farther and

farther away. I needed to get as much space between us as possible. Above me, the figure dangling from the parachute got smaller and smaller.

The plane came closer. I knew that plane. It was the one that Spike always flew.

There were maybe two thousand feet between us when I finally pulled my own rip cord.

One . . . two . . . three . . . Bang! My 'chute jerked me with the feeling of safety that I loved.

I fell at an angle. I had to twist to look past my 'chute at what was happening above.

It made me sick.

The airplane zoomed in on the parachute above me. Like a hawk closing in for the kill. It flew just over the parachute. Like a twist of smoke in wind, the parachute swirled and sucked. It wrapped around the small figure above me. There was no chance for the backup 'chute to open. No way to release the main parachute.

Then the figure grew as it gained speed.

Three seconds later, it fell past me. I didn't have to look up to watch it. I stared down as it dove toward the desert floor.

"Good-bye Sabella," I said. I knew I would never see her again.

Thirty seconds later, there was a little plop of dust. Just like in the roadrunner cartoons, when the coyote falls and falls and falls and finally hits.

From where I was, floating in the air, I saw it all.

A long black car started to speed out into the desert. Sabella's bodyguards.

But a brown car raced out from behind some brush in a gully. It cut the black car off. Two men jumped out of the brown car and waved the black car to a stop. It was the brown car that had followed me and Sabella from home. It was the brown car that had trapped me last night.

The FBI.

They were taking over the sudden, horrible death of Sabella Scanelli.

Chapter Eighteen

I went to Sabella's funeral two days later. Everyone from the flight school did. Everyone except for Spike. Spike was in jail. The FBI planned to charge him with the murder of Sabella Scanelli. Spike also confessed to wrecking her parachute on the day I saved her. But Spike was not telling them who hired him. Spike had wisely decided spending time in jail was better than getting murdered by the mob for squealing.

The funeral took place on a windy, rainy day. Las Vegas hardly has rainy days, but this was one of them. Gray weather for a gray day.

The gray matched the way I felt. Sad. I think Sabella and I might have become more than friends, but we'd never have the chance.

"Kid," a voice said to me. Ronnie Gold-Tooth stepped away from a bunch of other guys in suits. He stepped close to me and lowered his voice.

"Smart move on your part, kid. You see how the mob takes care of things? You make sure you keep your mouth shut."

"You too," I said. "The gold tooth looks stupid."

He frowned. Then he laughed.

"Brave, but stupid." He cuffed me across the head. "You're lucky I like you, kid."

I didn't like him.

He walked back to his friends. It would have been fun to tell him what the FBI guys had told me. Because of Mr. Scanelli's help, the FBI was ready to close in on a bunch of the mob. Mr. Scanelli was leaving the country tomorrow. The FBI would make the arrests as soon as Mr. Scanelli was safe.

I looked at the open sky that had been

such a friend to Sabella. I stood apart from the other flight school people. I listened to the quiet words of the preacher as the casket was lowered into the grave. It had been a closed casket funeral. Everyone knew that bodies don't look pretty after smashing into the ground from a mile high.

The preacher finished.

We began moving away.

A tall man in an expensive suit put his hand on my arm and stopped me.

"I'm Franco Scanelli," he said. The two bodyguards I had met in the desert stayed right at his elbows.

"Yes, sir," I said.

Mr. Scanelli had a lean, handsome face. I saw where Sabella had gotten her beauty.

"You're Jeff Nichols?"

"Yes, sir," I said.

"It's too bad we live in different worlds. From what I understand, it would be worth my while to know a fine young man like you."

I didn't know what to say to that.

He extended his hand. I took it. We shook.

"Nice to meet you," he said.

"Nice meeting you, sir."

We pulled our hands apart. He walked away with the two bodyguards. I stared after them.

I kept my right hand closed. Mr. Scanelli had slipped a piece of paper into it as we shook hands. He had taken a big risk to do that with so many Mafia guys around. The least I could do was wait until I got away from the funeral to read it.

Chapter Nineteen

I rode my motorcycle far out into the desert. Riding with the wind in my face on the wide open flats feels nearly as free as sky-diving. I didn't want to open the note. I had a good guess who had written it. I didn't know if I was ready for it. If it was more than good-bye, I would be sad. If it was less than good-bye, I would be sad.

Finally, at the end of a lonely stretch of two-lane highway, I pulled over. I set my helmet against a big rock. I sat on my helmet and leaned back against the rock.

I opened the note.

I was right. It was from Sabella Scanelli.

Jeff, if you're wondering how all this got started, it's because I watched you for a long time at the flight school. We never talked much. I couldn't. They don't let birds out of gold cages. But I saw how you are. I always wanted to talk to you and get to know you. That's why I came to your house for a ride to the flight school. If anyone would help, it was you. I really wanted to ask you for help, but at the last minute, I changed my mind. I didn't want you to get hurt.

But you helped anyway. And because you helped, I may never see you again. Leaving the money and the mansion is not the worst part of starting a new life. I hated that cage. The worst part is not having a chance to see you again.

I'm sorry.

Thanks for setting me free.

I folded the paper and stared at the sky. No, Sabella couldn't return. To the mob, she was dead. They could never find out she was alive. They could never find out how we had fooled them.

I'd jumped with a dummy dressed in Sabella's flight suit. The dummy was filled with rocks so it would fall like a real person.

The night before, when I'd talked to the FBI, we had come up with the plan. After the dummy hit the ground, the FBI guys stopped the bodyguards from seeing it.

Sabella had stayed hidden in the airplane. Not even Smitty knew she was there. Smitty landed and heard that Sabella had died. There was so much confusion that it had been easy for other FBI guys to sneak her away in a delivery truck.

I don't know, of course, how she had managed to get the note to Mr. Scanelli. Maybe the FBI had helped. Maybe she'd found another way. It was a chance on her part. The mob could never find out she was alive. I was happy she had taken the chance for me. Happy the note had been more than a simple good-bye.

And sad. I would never see her again.

I ripped up the note and let it float away in the desert wind. The pieces of paper dipped and rose in the wind. Almost like birds. Flying from an opened cage.

And Now, a Word from the Author ...

Dear Reader:

I wrote 'Chute Roll without any goal except to tell a story as well as I could. When I finished, I noticed that both Jeff Nichols and Sabella Scanelli kept mentioning freedom.

And freedom *is* a big deal. We all like to do what we want, when we want, and how we want. We know, however, that life can't always be that way. No matter how old we are, we have jobs and duties that tie us down. So we find freedom in many different ways.

Jeff and Sabella loved the freedom from

gravity. They felt like birds. While they were in the sky, they were free.

Maybe your freedom comes when you race a mountain bike down a hill. Or when you do in-line skating. Or when you get lost in a movie or a book.

But, like Jeff and Sabella, we have to land.

I think an interesting question is this: Why does something inside us want to be free?

The answer that I keep coming back to is a simple one. We are each born with a soul. It is as much a part of us as our mind and body. Our soul is invisible and cannot be held or touched or measured. Our soul, or spirit, longs for things that cannot be held or touched or measured. Like love or peace. Or freedom.

The greatest freedom is freedom of the spirit.

Our bodies don't have freedom. And won't, ever. We can't soar on the wind. We can't cut through water like a shark. Our bodies become sick. Sometimes our bodies heal. Sometimes they don't. Our bodies grow old and wear out.

But if you look beyond the limits of our

bodies, and think of the spirit's freedom, then there is hope. Nothing on earth, not even death, is so terrible that it can take away the freedom of our spirit.

Our soul is more important than our body. By instinct it longs for something better. That's what keeps us aimed toward God. And with that understanding, all of life's troubles are much easier to face.

After all, who wants to be a bird in a cage?

From your friend,

Sigmund Brouwer

Read and collect all of
Sigmund Brouwer's

SHORT
cuts
S E R I E S™

Turn the page for an exciting preview of

SCUBA DIVING
... to the Extreme:

Off the Wall

Ian Hill thinks it's going to be another boring summer helping his uncle run a scuba diving shop. Then, Ian hears that a storm has uncovered a pirate shipwreck hidden for years on the ocean floor. Soon Ian's slow summer at the scuba shop turns into a diver's nightmare.

At 70 feet deep in the water, I swallowed hard and popped my ears, something I had been doing all the way down. I did this to keep my eardrums from exploding.

At 75 feet, the ship below me was as big as a football field. I was only a few minutes away from it. It seemed ghostly in the dim water.

I finally reached the shipwreck at 100 feet. I found a place to hide the treasure chest and began to rise again.

It happened fifteen minutes later on my way up. At 53 feet deep, something ripped my mouthpiece away from my face and the water around me exploded.

I was still attached to the cable that was my guideline. For a couple of seconds, I bucked and danced at the end of my line. I felt like a rag doll shaken by a giant. Air bubbles kept exploding around my face mask. I grabbed my backup mouthpiece. It didn't work!

I tried to grab the main mouthpiece. At least it had air. The rubber tube was like a live snake. It twisted and turned in the water, trying to get away from me.

The air bubbles were coming from the mouthpiece. Air is squeezed into tanks under great pressure—3,000 pounds per square inch. A valve lets the air out slowly when you breathe. But the valve must have broken. The pressure was escaping, all at once. It was escaping through my mouthpiece—in a hurry. I was losing so much air and losing it so fast that the force of it was shaking my entire body.

I finally got my hands around the mouthpiece tube. I pulled the mouthpiece toward me. But there was no way I could put it back into my mouth. The air was shooting out too hard. Trying to breathe air from it would have been like trying to sip water from a fire hose.

But I needed air. Badly. And soon. I was 53 feet under water.

There was only one thing to do.

I unsnapped myself from the guideline. I dropped my weight belt and kicked upward. Already I wanted to suck for air. But I forced myself to breathe out instead. My only chance was to keep pushing air out of my lungs.

I kicked more. I kept pushing air out of my lungs. My body screamed at me. It wanted all the air it could get. But if I held my breath, my lungs would rip.

Higher and higher. Second after second. I kept breathing out, kept pushing air out of my starving lungs.

Just like a cork, I began moving faster and

faster. There was still air in my diving vest. I had pumped it in on my way down. That air was taking me higher and faster.

I felt something punch at my chest. It was an air pocket in the vest. It blew apart as the air inside it expanded. It reminded me to keep pushing air out of my lungs, no matter what.

My sight became fuzzy and black around the edges. I needed air so badly I was about to pass out. But if I did, my body would try to breathe. My lungs would suck in water, not air.

The water grew brighter and brighter. Would I make it to the surface in time?

Then I remembered.

The boat!

If I was going straight up, I would hit the boat. Like a cork popping out of water. But corks don't have skulls that can be smashed. I did.

With my last energy, I kicked with my legs, trying to move sideways as I rose. I kicked. Kicked. Kicked . . .

**For more exciting sports stories
don't miss**

SIGMUND BROUWER'S

SERIES

Each book weaves a tantalizing
sports mystery that includes plenty
of on-ice hockey drama.